DISNEY
THE NUTCRACKER
AND THE
FOUR REALMS

Read-Along
STORYBOOK AND CD

Clara is transported into a strange and mysterious world where she meets a soldier named Phillip, a gang of mice, and regents who preside over the Realms. To find out what happens, read along with me in your book. You will know it's time to turn the page when you hear this sound. . . . Let's begin now.

DISNEY PRESS
LOS ANGELES • NEW YORK

Printed in the United States of America

First Paperback Edition, September 2018

1 3 5 7 9 10 8 6 4 2

ISBN 978-1-368-02586-7

FAC-038091-18235

For more Disney Press fun, visit www.disneybooks.com

SUSTAINABLE FORESTRY INITIATIVE
Certified Sourcing
www.sfiprogram.org
SFI-00993
Logo Applies to Text Stock Only

It was Christmas Eve in London, and Charles Stahlbaum was trying to appear cheerful. "Now, children, I have some presents for you." Less than a year had passed since they'd lost their mother, and they were missing her dearly. He explained the gifts were from her. "She asked me to give them to you on Christmas Eve. So."

Fritz, the youngest, tore open his gift of ten tin soldiers. Louise, the oldest, was given her mother's favorite dress. Mr. Stahlbaum turned to his other daughter as she reluctantly opened her present.

"It's an egg of some sort. I think it opens." The family looked on curiously as Clara tried to open it. "It's locked." She rummaged through the wrapping, searching for a key, but found only a note from her mother. She hurried upstairs with the note in hand.

It read, *To my beautiful Clara. Everything you need is inside. Love, Mother.*

Clara picked up a small magnifying glass from her desk and inspected the lock as her father walked in. "This is a pin-tumbler lock. It's impossible to open without a key."

"I see. Well, why don't you get ready for the party and you can work it out tomorrow?"

"I don't want to go to the party."

Mr. Stahlbaum told her that was not an option. "Yes, but it's important to maintain traditions as a family. It's what's expected of us."

As her sister helped her get ready, Clara examined the egg. She turned it over and noticed an engraved letter D. "Drosselmeyer! Godfather must have made this. That means . . . maybe he can open it!"

Later that evening, when the family climbed into the carriage and left for Drosselmeyer's holiday party, Clara brought the egg along.

On their way, Mr. Stahlbaum reminded the children to be on their best behavior. "And I expect one dance with you, Louise. And you, Clara."

"Do I have to dance—"

"Yes, you do. And no disappearing tonight, Clara."

Clara hung her head. "Yes, Father."

They entered Drosselmeyer's grand home to find the great hall bursting with cheer. Guests danced around a towering Christmas tree glittering with ornaments and lights. Clara pushed through the crowd and began searching for her godfather.

She found him in his workshop. "Backwards. It moves backwards." He turned the swan toy on to demonstrate.

Clara unscrewed one of the parts, inspecting it. "It looks like the idler wheel has slipped." She used her tools to fix it.

"Clever girl!"

When she revealed the egg, Drosselmeyer smiled. "I haven't seen this in a long, long time." But he couldn't help—the lock was too difficult to pick.

When the clock chimed, Drosselmeyer grinned. "You run along, and I'll be up shortly."

Mr. Stahlbaum frowned when he saw Clara. "I told you not to disappear. And I was expecting to dance with you."

"I *really* don't want to dance."

"Why, Clara, must you think only about yourself?"

"I could ask you the same thing."

Hurt, he walked away.

Out in the garden, strings were woven through statues and branches. Each strand had a name on one end and a gift from Drosselmeyer on the other. Clara found her name and followed the string. It wound back into the house, through narrow hallways and dark rooms . . .

And finally to a snow-covered forest! Clara continued until she saw the string's end—where a key glittered, deep within the branches of an enormous tree. She knew it must be her missing key! "Clever Godfather."

As she reached for it, a mouse scampered up the trunk and snatched it!

"Hey! That's mine." Clara chased the mouse deep into the woods until it ran over a frozen river. She carefully stepped onto it, and the ice cracked.

She hurried toward a nearby footbridge, and a nutcracker soldier standing guard came to life. "Halt!" When he learned Clara's name, he bowed. "You're the daughter of Queen Marie?" He leaped up, standing at attention. "Captain Phillip Hoffman, Your Majesty!"

Clara explained that she had to get across the bridge.

"Are you certain, Princess Clara? The Fourth Realm is a very dangerous place."

"Yes, I'm certain. Please call me Clara."

As Phillip escorted her, Clara told him about the key. When she spotted the mouse, she chased it until it disappeared into a tree stump. "Come on out of there!"

Behind her, a giant figure emerged from the fog. Clara tried to run, but it grabbed her. "Aaaahhh!" The monster was made of thousands of mice swarming together. The mouse with her key was at the very top!

Phillip grabbed Clara and managed to pull her from the monster's grip. It immediately began chasing them.

"Run! It's the Mouse King!"

As they escaped, trees fell, blocking their path, and a voice boomed. "I have your key. . . ." An enormous silhouette towered above.

"It's a trap! If you go, you'll never come back. No one ever does!" Clara glanced behind her as she and Phillip raced away.

"*That* was Mother Ginger." Phillip explained that she was the evil ruler of the Fourth Realm.

Moments later, Phillip took Clara to a palace to meet the regents. The Regent of the Land of Sweets, Sugar Plum, beamed with happiness. "I never thought this day would come."

They were saddened to hear that Marie had died and asked Clara if she'd come to take over her mother's crown and save them from Mother Ginger.

"No. I'm sorry. I didn't even know this place existed before today."

To celebrate Clara's arrival, the regents decided to throw a pageant.

Sugar Plum showed Clara around. As they walked through the palace, Clara asked about Mother Ginger. Sugar Plum explained that she had been a regent before she was banished. "She wanted to take control of the other realms by force. But when her evil intentions were made clear, even her own people deserted her, and her realm fell to ruin."

Sugar Plum led Clara to a rotating platform. They rose up, and through the glass they could see Drosselmeyer's party—they were *inside* the grandfather clock!

Clara marveled at the sight. "Everything is going so slowly."

"Your world moves much more slowly than our world."

Clara spotted her father sitting alone, sadly. "I haven't seen him like that before."

"Everything looks different from the Realms."

Sugar Plum then led Clara to a lavish bedroom. "Your mother's room." She showed her a wardrobe full of beautiful dresses.

"I'm not very good at dresses . . . shoes . . . hair . . ."

Sugar Plum helped Clara get ready and made her look like a princess.

Everyone cheered as Clara entered the palace auditorium. Sugar Plum smiled. "You are every inch your mother's daughter."

A beautiful ballerina took the stage and the show began. Sugar Plum leaned over to Clara. "The pageant tells the story of the Four Realms—how your mother created our world."

Clara was stunned. "My mother made all of this?"

"She wasn't just our queen. She was our creator."

The ballerina danced as flowers bloomed, snow fell, and sweets appeared. Clara was completely mesmerized.

"First, your mother created the Land of Flowers. Next she created the Land of Snowflakes."

"And the Land of Sweets?"

"I'll show you!"

The pageant ended and everyone rose, applauding wildly.

Moments later Sugar Plum led Clara down a staircase. She explained that they had all been toys before Marie gave them life.

She opened a heavy door and revealed a messy workshop. A tube connected to a complex machine sat at its center. "The Engine."

Sugar Plum told Clara that Mother Ginger was gathering her forces. "It must be because you're here, dear Clara. As Queen Marie's rightful heir, your very presence is a threat to her."

"There must be something we can do."

"The Engine is the only way that we can build an army to defend ourselves." Sugar Plum explained that the machine wasn't working—they were missing the key.

Clara inspected the keyhole on the Engine and the one on her egg. "The locks are the same. The key must be the same." She knew she had to go back to the Fourth Realm. They warned her of the danger, but Clara insisted. "I have to try. I must get that key!"

In the morning, Phillip and Clara led a troop of soldiers out of the courtyard and across the drawbridge.

As they entered the Fourth Realm, the air became thick with fog and the sounds of mice echoed around them.

"It's the mice! They're under us!" They tried to escape. Soldiers began disappearing, falling into mouseholes. Clara jumped over one of the holes but slipped into another. "No!" She fell down and down until she landed on a carpet of mice! "Phillip!"

The mice carried her through a tunnel and up into the fog.

"I've been expecting you." Mother Ginger scooped Clara up with her enormous hand. Clara told her she had come for the key, and Mother Ginger swooshed her beneath her tentlike skirt. Polichinelles appeared and began dancing and flipping, creating a chaotic storm around Clara, forcing her to sit on a chair. They pulled a lever, sending the chair spinning around a pole and speeding upward. Once it stopped, Clara found herself inside a circular room with levers, knobs, and dials. She realized she was in the body of the giant doll.

Clara spotted the key just as a woman appeared. "Hands off, young lady."

"You're Mother Ginger?"

"And you're Queen Marie's daughter."

As Clara reached for the key, Mother Ginger pulled levers to make the doll lean, causing Clara to tumble.

"You're trying to destroy everything my mother ever created."

"That's what sweet Sugar Plum's been telling you, is it?"

For a moment, Clara wondered what Mother Ginger meant, but she had no time to waste. She swiftly maneuvered the levers to control the doll and swipe the key!

She met up with Phillip and they ran into the woods. When they were safe, Clara used the key to open the egg. "It's just a music box!" She couldn't believe it. "My mother told me everything I needed was inside." Clara told Phillip she felt just as lost as she had before.

Phillip turned to Clara. "You led a regiment of men into the Fourth Realm and took back this key from Mother Ginger. You're not lost, Clara Stahlbaum. Your place is here."

Clara smiled. "Let's go."

Clara and Phillip made it safely back to the palace. Sugar Plum was delighted to see that they had succeeded and hurried to try the key. Cogs and belts whirred and whizzed as the machine came to life. "Wonderful! Bring me the tin soldiers!"

Sugar Plum turned up all the levels, and the soldiers whipped through the machinery, coming out the other end alive—and seven feet tall! "Prepare to march on the Fourth Realm!"

Clara and Phillip were shocked to hear that she wanted to invade. "But my mother would have never wanted this—"

"I don't care what your mother wanted!"

Something dawned on Clara. "Mother Ginger didn't do anything wrong, did she? You lied to me, to everyone!"

Sugar Plum smiled wickedly. "I have a very special plan for Mother Ginger and the other regents." She told one of the guards to stand in the middle of the machine. Then she pushed a button, and he was zapped back into a lifeless doll! She ordered the guards to take Clara and Phillip away.

The guards locked them inside a tower. Clara sat down and pulled out her egg. She opened it and poked at the inside of the lid. It rotated, revealing a mirror. Clara suddenly knew what her mother's message meant. "It's me. That's what was inside."

Phillip looked up at her, confused.

"She was talking about *me*." Clara, full of energy, quickly began to devise a plan to stop Sugar Plum's army.

Clara and Phillip cleverly lowered themselves to the balcony below and walked along a ledge, eyeing the soldiers marching toward the Fourth Realm. They made their way to the courtyard and climbed through a hatch. Soon they stood on a cliff facing a roaring waterfall!

Clara knew what to do. "You have to warn Mother Ginger."

They wished each other luck, and Clara began to carefully climb down the wet, rocky ledge toward the Engine Room.

Clara made her way inside, but the soldiers soon found her there. To her surprise, Mother Ginger arrived to help. "At your service, Your Majesty!" She battled the wicked soldiers as Clara tried to disable the machine.

Sugar Plum, realizing someone was in the Engine Room, hurried inside. "Mother Ginger! I'm just so pleased you decided to drop in!" Clara remained hidden as Sugar Plum tied Mother Ginger up and turned on the contraption before Clara disabled it!

Clara eyed a pin in the machinery and came up with a new idea. She worked quickly as Sugar Plum barked at the soldiers. "Put her on the platform!"

Clara moved the pin and stood up. "Sugar Plum, stop!" She tried to convince Sugar Plum to change her mind, but the regent's selfish goals prevailed, and she pushed the button.

Without the pin in place, the mechanism moved—and aimed directly at Sugar Plum! "Oh, shhhhhhhh . . . ugar." In a flash, Sugar Plum turned back into a doll.

In the wake of Clara's victory over the wicked Sugar Plum, the Four Realms gathered to celebrate her as their hero. Mother Ginger was reinstated as the Regent of the Fourth Realm. They wanted Clara to stay and be their queen, but she had to return to her family, and she knew they didn't truly need a queen. "Everything you need is already inside. That's what my mother knew. And now, in her absence, you must all support each other. Work to forge a new future. Together."

Later, Phillip escorted Clara through the snowy forest. "Please come back to the Realms one day."

"Of course I will."

Clara walked beyond the forest through a dark passage and opened a door. She found her godfather in the great hall. "There you are. Back so soon?"

"Godfather, you never told me she created all that!"

Drosselmeyer's eyes twinkled brightly. "Clara, your mother was the cleverest inventor I ever knew. But there was never any doubt when I asked her what her greatest invention was: you."

Clara returned to the party and found her father, alone. They talked about how much they missed her mother.

"We are lucky, Father. To have each other."

"Yes, that's right." They hugged tightly. "Shall we go home?"

"Don't you owe me a dance first?"

Clara opened the egg. As its lovely tune played, Mr. Stahlbaum's face lit up. "That is the song that your mother and I first danced to."

They waltzed, and soon Louise and Fritz joined them. From a window above, Drosselmeyer smiled as he watched the happy family dance together.